Meet Me in Dreamland

A Good Night Tale

By Steven & Valerie McKinney   Illustrated by Jarmila Dicova-Ondrejkova

JOHN JASPER BOOKS, An Imprint of MetroDigi, Inc, Ross, California and UNUS BOOKS, A Division of Unus LLC, Mountain Brook, Alabama

Lu-Chu in Shanghai prepared for day's end.

She hopped into bed to dream of her friend.

Lena in Springfield, her toes warm and tight,

was excited to dream of Lu-Chu tonight.

The girls had found each other on a river cruise, sensing something special over how-do-you-do's.

They played in the park with their Chinese kites, giggling and wiggling in friendship's delight.

Lu-Chu told Lena how she runs through the park,

while her dog runs behind her with a joyful bark.

Lena said, "I play outdoors, too, under a tree.

It seems that you like all the same things as me!"

Lu-Chu said, "Oh, yes. And when there's a breeze,

I love how the leaves swirl down from the trees."

"Me too!" cried Lena. "And it's so much fun

to try to catch them. I love to run!"

They swung to and fro from one story to another,

sharing their secrets with only each other.

Now alone in her bedroom, Lu-Chu's feeling sad.

She misses Lena and the fun they both had.

Now that she's home, Lena's feeling sad, too,

wishing that she could still be with Lu-Chu.

The playful memories dance in their heads,

making it hard to lie down in their beds.

Lena had shared a secret to put Lu-Chu at ease:

count branches, count leaves, or stars in the trees.

Their eyelids grow heavy, the numbers all spin,

and little by little, Dreamland draws them in.

For deep in Dreamland,

all cozy and tight,

the wonders of the day await you tonight.

The End

For our dear daughters,

Hana, Addison and Karolina

We'd like to express our gratitude to the following people without which this book would never have made it to print:

Summer Laurie, Carol Barkin, Lisa Hilgers, John McKinney, Stephen Chazen, David & Jan Ibarra, Frank Gaynor,

Peter Dic, Edward Walters, Dr. Stephen Stukovsky, Stefania Stukovsky and Dr. Stefan Stukovsky.

~Steven & Valerie McKinney

For information about permission to reproduce selections from this book, write to Permissions at:
JOHN JASPER BOOKS, AN IMPRINT OF METRODIGI, INC.   PO Box 1789, Ross, California 94957
UNUS BOOKS, A DIVISION OF UNUS LLC   Mountain Brook, Alabama 35253

www.johnjasperbooks.com

ISBN 978-0-9844272-3-9

Manufactured in China